TROLL
D0245558

9 39667475

Titles in Teen Reads:

BILLY BUTTON
CAVAN SCOTT

DAWN OF THE DAVES
TIM COLLINS

DEAD SCARED
TOMMY DONBAVAND

DEADLY MISSION
MARK WRIGHT

FAIR GAME
ALAN DURANT

JIGSAW LADY
TONY LEE

HOME
TOMMY DONBAVAND

KIDNAP
TOMMY DONBAVAND

MAMA BARKFINGERS
CAVAN SCOTT

PEST CONTROL
CAVAN SCOTT

SITTING TARGET
JOHN TOWNSEND

STALKER
TONY LEE

THE HUNTED
CAVAN SCOTT

THE CORRIDOR
MARK WRIGHT

TROLL
TIM COLLINS

UNDERWORLD
SIMON CHESHIRE

WARD 13
TOMMY DONBAVAND

WORLD WITHOUT WORDS
JONNY ZUCKER

Badger Publishing Limited, Oldmedow Road, Hardwick Industrial Estate, King's Lynn PE30 4JJ
Telephone: 01438 791037

www.badgerlearning.co.uk

TROLL

TIM COLLINS

Troll ISBN 978-1-78147-807-3

Publisher: Susan Ross
Senior Editor: Danny Pearson
Publishing Assistant: Claire Morgan
Copyeditor: Cheryl Lanyon
Designer: Bigtop Design Ltd

2 4 6 8 10 9 7 5 3 1

CHAPTER 1

THREAT

I will find you.

I will hurt you.

Alice had deleted the posts and blocked the person who'd sent them. But she couldn't stop thinking about them.

I will come after you.

I will make your life hell.

She plonked down on the bench opposite the science block and took her battered phone out of her pocket.

I am watching you.

You'll see me soon.

Her pulse sped as she spotted a blood-red circle in the top right corner of the Facebook icon. Was her troll back?

No. It was just her dad. He'd liked the picture she'd posted on Sunday. He hadn't commented, though. And he still hadn't replied to her last text. But it was something.

You are empty.

You are a zero.

She'd heard nothing from her mysterious abuser since she'd blocked him, but she still felt a little nervous whenever she checked her phone or switched on her laptop at home.

A crowd of year tens was piling out of the science block, pushing past each other to get to the lunch queue. Could any of them be her troll?

The messages could have come from anyone.

But why would they have it in for her? She didn't have many friends except Chris, but she was sure she didn't have any enemies either.

She hated her dad's new girlfriend, Janet, but it wasn't mutual. Janet could barely remember her name. She'd never do anything like that.

This was just some dorky little loser, sitting alone in his bedroom, trying to upset her because it was the only way he could get a response out of anyone.

Best to ignore it. It was like they said – never feed the trolls.

Alice was scrolling down her news feed when her phone buzzed.

A new text. Finally her dad had replied to her.

She tapped the messages icon. This wasn't from her dad. In fact, she didn't recognise the number at all. Alice read the text and her heart raced.

You are worthless. You are nothing. I will hurt you.

CHAPTER 2

LAIR

"This is it," said Chris, pointing at the dark office building.

They were outside a door coated with flaking white paint in the middle of a deserted industrial estate. The letterbox was stuffed with envelopes, some of which had fallen to the floor. A faded sign next to the buzzer said 'The Bridge Company'.

When Alice had told Chris about the text, he'd traced the number online and found the exact location it had been sent from. She'd been expecting a semi-detached suburban house, not an abandoned office.

Light was draining out of the sky. Streetlamps pinged on along the empty street and the distant main road where the bus had dropped them off. The grey concrete of the buildings was fading into darkness.

Alice wandered over to a large window to the right of the door. She could make out an abandoned office through the saggy, white blinds. There was a desk in the far corner, but no other furniture.

"There's no one here," said Alice.

"Maybe the little dweeb's hiding from you," said Chris. "It's no wonder. He's probably never spoken to an actual girl before."

Chris pressed the buzzer and a shrill electric scream echoed around the empty building.

Nothing stirred.

He tried the white plastic handle and the door creaked open.

"Hello?" he shouted. "Are you in there, loser?"

Alice peered over Chris's shoulder into the dark corridor. She wondered if her troll really was just some loser. He'd certainly gone to a lot of effort to stay under cover.

Chris stepped inside and tried the light switch. Nothing. Alice thought the building must have been abandoned for a long time.

He disappeared into the murky corridor. Alice followed, holding her phone out like a torch.

In its weak light, she could see Chris ducking into a doorway on the right.

Alice went in after him. This was the office she'd spied through the window. The carpet was covered in dark coffee splodges and imprints of old furniture. There were two rusty metal pillars in the middle of the room and dirty white panels were hanging down from the ceiling.

The air was filled with a stale, damp smell, and thick dust was swirling in the glow of her phone.

Chris walked over to the desk at the far wall.

"Any clues?" asked Alice.

"Maybe," said Chris. "Look at these."

Through the deep gloom, Alice could see pictures taped to the wall.

She approached them, fearing they'd be photos of dead bodies taken in this room. Maybe the dark stains weren't coffee after all? The troll had threatened to hurt her. Maybe he carried out his threats.

Her mind suggested an even darker possibility. What if they were pictures of her? Snapshots taken from behind bushes, blurry images of her bedroom window…?

They were nothing of the sort. Alice swept the light of her phone over the pictures and saw they were just magazine clippings. They showed glum-looking, middle-aged women on sofas staring into the camera, with headlines like:

'He cheated while I was EIGHT months pregnant'

'Hubby had SECRET BABY with my best friend'

'He tried to make me KILL my child'

Alice had seen these sorts of sob stories before. There were loads in her mum's magazines. They let you spy on the misery of others and forget your own troubles for a while. Entertaining in a guilty sort of way. But why would someone make a shrine to them?

One of the articles had the headline, **'My STALKER hell'**. Some words had been circled in red: 'He said I was worthless, that I was nothing and that he was going to hurt me.'

e are the same words he sent me," said
ce. "This proves we've found the right guy."

The front door creaked open and heavy footsteps thudded down the corridor.

Alice crouched behind the desk and Chris ducked down next to her.

The footsteps stomped nearer. Alice could hear loud snorting. It sounded more like a bull than a human.

She peered round the desk and saw a huge man wearing a wide-brimmed hat and a long, black leather coat.

So much for her idea about the bedroom wimp. This was one of the tallest and strongest-looking men she'd ever seen. His thick arms were almost bursting the seams of his sleeves.

Alice couldn't see the man's face under the shadow of his hat, but she glimpsed his profile and saw he had a long, droopy nose. She wondered if he'd been teased about it as a child and that's what had made him so angry with the world.

The man stopped in the middle of the room and sniffed in short, noisy bursts.

He glanced over to the table and Alice ducked back behind it. Chris was staring at her with wide eyes.

Alice heard the man striding over, sniffing as he walked. She could see the shadow of his huge frame on the wall behind the desk. Thick legs appeared next to her, wafting trails of dust.

Alice sneezed.

The dark figure crouched down.

"You!" said the man. His voice sounded like a recording that had been slowed down. "You came here?"

He let out a deep chuckle. "Well, this makes things easier."

He took a small, brown bottle out of his inside pocket and splashed something onto a scrap of cloth. He shoved it into Alice's face and a sharp smell filled her nostrils. The room blurred and her eyelids felt heavy.

CHAPTER 3

PRISONER

Alice opened her eyes. She was still in the office.

She was standing up, but couldn't move.

Her wrists were bound behind her back and cold metal was digging into her arms. She craned her neck and saw she'd been tied to one of the rusty pillars. She thrashed her head from side to side, sending pins and needles up her arms.

Chris was tied to the other pillar, a few feet along from her. His head was lolling to the right and his eyes were closed.

The man was standing in the middle of the room, flipping through a magazine.

"'Hubby tried to kill me on our wedding night,'" he muttered. "Excellent."

He tore the page out and threw it onto a pile on the floor.

Alice tried to scream, but could only manage a hoarse cry.

The man looked up.

"You're back," he said in his deep, slow voice. "Good."

"Why are you doing this to me?" asked Alice.

"Why?" replied the man, striding towards her. "Because you're fat and ugly and I hate you. Everyone does. I'm the only one honest enough to tell you."

Alice felt her cheeks flush. She'd never been called fat before. Maybe she was a little overweight. She'd eaten a lot at Christmas and hadn't really got rid of the weight yet…

Alice stopped herself. This was how people like this got under your skin. Let them get to you and they win.

The man stopped a few feet away. Alice peered at him, but could still see nothing under the shadow of his hat.

"You're nothing," he said. "A dead-eyed zombie, a mouth-breather, an oxygen thief."

The man's breath smelled like a stagnant, festering drain.

"It's no wonder your dad left," said the man.

Alice felt her pulse speed. How could he have known about that? She'd never mentioned it anywhere online. She'd hardly even told anyone at school.

"You're so special compared to all the others, aren't you?" sneered the man. "You're really going to be someone, right?"

He sniggered. "Nonsense! I've been around a long time, you know. I've seen it all before. Picture your mum sitting alone on the couch in her jogging pants, sobbing at soap operas. That'll be you in twenty years. Another lifeless husk in a faceless town waiting for the sweet release of death."

Alice blinked tears out of her eyes. What had she done to make this man so angry? She was sure she'd never met him before.

A car drove past, sending bright white stripes of light across the room. Alice caught a glimpse of the man's face for the first time.

His long nose drooped down over sharp teeth. His tiny black eyes were sunk into deep pits under his jutting brow. But weirder than any of this was his skin. It was as grey and rough as stone.

Alice felt her heart pounding. Her bully, her tormentor, her captor. He wasn't just an online troll. He was an actual troll.

CHAPTER 4

TROLL

"Your dad never wanted a child," said the troll. "You were nothing more than a burden to him. I'm amazed he stuck around as long as he did. But still you make demands on the poor man. You're so needy, so desperate to be loved. He complains to Janet every time you text him."

Alice's mind was racing. How could the monster possibly know the name of her dad's new girlfriend? And if it was right about Janet's name, could it be right about her dad? He always said he was pleased to see her, but he'd go days without replying to her texts. And he changed the subject whenever she asked if she could come and stay.

Alice's eyes were stinging. She blinked, and a hot tear ran down her cheek.

The creature reached out and scraped it away. Its rough skin felt like sandpaper on Alice's face.

The troll sniffed his finger and grinned. "Excellent," he said. "I knew it would be."

Chris murmured from the other pillar and the troll wandered over to him.

Alice remembered what the troll had said about her mum and she felt her cheeks flushing. What right did this stupid beast have to judge her mum? She was a good person, and she'd always been there for Alice.

She tried to stop herself. She needed to forget the troll's words and think straight. The creature had ranted at her until she'd started crying. Why was it so keen to upset her?

She glanced over at Chris. He was squirming against his ropes as the monster darted around and sniffed him.

"I bet you're so happy spending all that time on your computer," the troll was saying. "It must be great to have so many friends on Facebook. I wonder how many of them would come to your funeral if you died right now? Not many, I'm betting."

"Say what you like," said Chris. "I don't care."

"But you *do* care," said the troll, taking a deep sniff. "I can smell it. Because you know I'm telling the truth. You're lonely. You're an outcast. You're Billy-No-Mates."

Alice stared at the creature. It was over eight feet tall now, even larger than when she'd first seen it.

The monster lurched back to her.

"Still crying?" it asked. "You should be. Because you're nothing. You're a blank. You're a black hole."

This time she blocked it out.

Never feed the troll.

She thought this over and over again until the creature's words faded away. It soon padded back over to Chris.

"Don't listen!" she shouted. "Block it out!"

The creature started speaking again, but Chris closed his eyes.

"They all talk about you, you know. About how strange you are. Some of them pity you, but most of them hate you." The creature was yelling now, and dusty flecks of spit were landing on Chris's scrunched face.

The creature seemed to shrink a little. It was back to its original size, and its shoulders were slumping.

The troll growled and stomped out of the room, slamming the door behind it.

"What happened?" asked Chris.

"I think it feeds off anguish," said Alice. "It needs it to survive. That's why it reads all those magazine sob stories. When we were upset, it got taller and stronger, but when we ignored it, it got smaller and weaker."

Alice could hear the muffled voice of the troll coming from a room above them. It seemed to be on the phone, and she could only make out what it was saying when it raised its voice.

"I will come after you! I will hurt you!"

"It's getting its strength up again," said Alice. "We need to get out of here."

Alice tried to free her hands from the ropes, but they were too tight. She craned round and examined the pillar.

The metal near the bottom had rusted away, creating a jagged edge. She wriggled down to the ground. Her shoulders twisted painfully behind her back, and she let out a low cry. She rubbed the rope up and down on the sharp metal until her arms throbbed.

Tiny shards of rust dug into her skin as she dragged the rope over the crooked metal.

Finally, the rope snapped.

She collapsed to the floor and rubbed her numb wrists together.

"Great," said Chris. "Now untie me."

"Give me a second," said Alice.

She scrunched her hands into fists and some of the numbness went away. She hobbled over to Chris and grasped the ropes. Her arms were weak, as if she'd fallen asleep on them, and it was difficult to get a grip.

The troll had gone quiet upstairs.

"Hurry," said Chris.

Finally, a tiny gap opened in the knot. Alice tugged the ropes and they fell away. She could hear the troll stomping in the room above.

It was coming back.

CHAPTER 5

ESCAPE

Alice ran down the deserted street. Chris was ahead of her, speeding through the circles of light thrown by the sparse streetlamps.

They'd managed to crawl out of a back window, just as the troll had returned. They'd scrabbled up a steep grass verge and found themselves on a street that sloped up to the main road.

Alice glanced over her shoulder. A large figure was lumbering through the pools of light behind them. The troll was coming.

She forced herself to go faster, ignoring the sharp pain in her side.

The bright main road was ahead. It was lined with streetlamps on both sides and a few cars were passing. Surely one of them would stop and help.

Two lights appeared around the corner. A bus.

Alice glanced left. There was a bus stop on her side of the road, about a hundred metres away. Chris was pelting towards it. She did her best to keep up, forcing herself to go faster.

The troll was closing in. Alice could see its dark outline flitting through the lights behind her. Clouds of dust were curling up as it passed.

The bus was almost level and the stop was too far away. They weren't going to make it.

Chris lurched into the path of the bus, waving his arms above his head. It skidded to a halt, and Alice heard angry shouts from inside.

The troll was almost upon her. A strong, rough hand would clasp her shoulder at any moment.

Chris was at the side of the bus, banging the doors. They opened with a mechanical sigh and he rushed in.

“What are you doing?” shouted the driver, a bald man with cracked red cheeks. “You could have got yourself killed.”

Alice raced towards the open door. She could hear the thud of the creature behind her.

CHAPTER 6

INTRUDER

Alice squinted at the shapes on the whiteboard. Mr Byrne had closed the curtains and dimmed the lights to use the projector, and she was struggling to keep her eyes open.

She felt her lids close, but an image of the troll's grey skin and vicious black eyes jolted her awake again.

As the bus had pulled away the night before, the dark figure of the creature had sunk back into the murk. She'd been able to make out its outline falling into the distance as the bus had sped off.

She'd been expecting it to pounce as she ran back to her house from her bus stop, but nothing had happened.

She'd slept fitfully, waking up every few minutes to imagine the creature was standing at the end of her bed, sniffing and grinning.

But now she was sitting in the warm classroom and scribbling in her textbook, she was starting to think she'd imagined it all.

She probably wouldn't believe it if Chris weren't sitting next to her.

"We need to tell the police," he said.

"Tell them what?" asked Alice. "That we were attacked by a creature from a fairytale?"

"Concentrate," said Mr Byrne, turning away from the whiteboard and looking at them. The projector was reflecting off his glasses, making him look like he had huge, white eyes.

"It'll go after someone else if we don't," whispered Chris. "It might even come back for us."

Alice sighed and took her phone out. She pressed nine three times, but couldn't make herself press 'call'.

"Let's wait and see," she said, putting her phone back in her pocket. "For all we know, we might never hear from it again."

A scream rang out from the playground. Chairs scraped over the floor and everyone scrabbled for the windows. The curtains were yanked aside and light flooded in.

"Sit down," said Mr Byrne, wincing at the daylight. "I'm sure there's nothing to see."

Alice hoped a fight had broken out, or a stray dog had wandered into the playground.

"There was a man in a long coat and hat," Sally Jones said. "He pushed one of the year sevens over."

Alice's heart raced. It had tracked her here. And if it had tracked her here, she'd never be able to escape it.

Screams were echoing from the stairwell. Alice could hear footsteps and sniffs getting louder and louder.

The door swung open and the troll appeared. A thin plume of dust drifted in, followed by the stale smell of the empty office. The troll fixed its small black eyes on Alice and grinned.

CHAPTER 7

ATTACK

Mr Byrne stepped into the path of the troll, but it batted him aside. The teacher caught his back on the corner of his desk and tumbled to the floor. His glasses fell off and one of the lenses popped out.

The creature lurched over to him and took a long sniff.

"Your wife doesn't love you," it said. "She wasn't working late last night. She was with your brother, Michael."

Mr Byrne looked at the creature and whimpered. He gathered the remains of his glasses and hobbled out.

Everyone crowded after him, streaming down the sides of the room to keep their distance from the monster.

The creature grabbed Seema Ahmed by the arm. It sniffed her head and said, "Your brother is never going to get better."

It released her and she darted out of the room, wiping tears from her eyes.

It grabbed the shoulder of a boy called Shane Harris and sniffed him. "Your dad isn't on an oilrig. He's in prison."

"You're lying!" shouted Shaun. He squirmed free and fled to the door, his cheeks flushing red.

"Leave them," said Alice. "It's me you want."

"Of course it's you I want," said the creature. "Your grief is among the finest I've ever experienced. And that was just from our silly little game in the office. Imagine how intoxicating it will be when I take you far away and you realise you'll be alone forever."

Alice's heart sank as she noticed the entire classroom was empty. Even Chris had fled.

"Of course he's gone," said the troll. "He's not your friend. You don't have any friends."

Alice flung herself down and sheltered behind her desk. The troll was trying to peer into her thoughts. She needed to control them.

The creature yanked the desk up and threw it across the room. It smashed above the doorway, splintering into sharp chunks of wood.

"I'm not surprised," said the troll. "I wouldn't be your friend. What have you got to offer? You're nothing. No one will miss you when I take you away."

Alice covered her head with her hands.

Never feed the troll, she thought to herself.

"That's what's going to happen, you see," said the troll. "I'm going to take you to a place where no one will ever find you and I'm going to wallow in your suffering. I'm going to keep you alive just to enjoy your misery. You'll want to die, of course. You'll beg for death. But I'll never grant your wish."

Alice blinked and felt tears welling in her eyes.

Never feed the troll.

She repeated it over and over again, blocking out the monster as it ranted.

Never feed the troll.

She glanced up at the creature. It was towering over her, taking long, deep breaths.

Alice thought she could see something moving behind it, but her vision was blurred by tears.

She rubbed her eyes.

Chris was coming. He'd picked up a long, sharp shard of wood and was creeping towards the monster.

Alice felt her heart lift, but she remembered how the monster could sense her thoughts. She'd have to disguise them to give Chris a chance.

I am worthless, she thought. She said the words slowly and clearly in the front of her mind.

I am ugly, she thought. Chris was inching silently towards the monster and she fought against rising hope.

I am stupid, she thought. The shard of wood was right behind the creature now.

"That's right," said the troll. "I'm so glad you understand."

I am brilliant, she thought.

The troll's thick brow furrowed.

Alice sprang up and shoved the creature hard in the chest. It plunged back onto the shard. The sharp wood ripped through its body and poked out of its stomach.

"You're the worthless one," shouted Alice. "You're the ugly one. And you're definitely the stupid one."

The troll screamed. It looked down and clawed the end of the shard, shedding splintery chunks onto the floor.

The creature's hands fell limp. It dropped to its knees and gazed at Alice. It opened its mouth, but no scream came out.

Its face froze. Specks of dust drifted from its skin, making it rough and uneven, like a weather-beaten statue.

Dust was thickening the air. Through the haze, Alice could see the monster's black eyes and white teeth turning as grey as its skin. Larger chunks were crumbling away now. The end of its nose dropped to the floor, followed by the top of its ear.

Alice walked over to the creature and poked its forehead. The top half of its face slid away and shattered into chunks on the floor.

Chris picked up one of the chunks and it crumbled apart.

"I thought you'd gone," said Alice. "I thought you'd left me to fight it alone."

"Of course not," said Chris. "I was looking for something to attack it with. I'm glad it smashed that desk because this was the only other thing I could find."

He took a small metal ruler out of his pocket.

"I don't think that would have done much damage," said Alice.

"I know," said Chris. "But I'd have tried."

CHAPTER 8

AFTER

Chris was waiting on the bench outside the science block. Alice sat down next to him and grasped his hand.

Just over a week later, it seemed impossible that any of it could have happened.

No one in the school ever mentioned it. Shortly after Alice had scooped the dusty remains of the troll out of the window, Mr Byrne had rushed back into the room. He was wearing his glasses again, though the right lens was missing.

"The intruder's escaped through the fire exit," he'd said. "I tried to catch him, but he got away."

"Really?" Alice had asked. "I hope they track him down."

She'd gone along with the official story in the police interviews. A madman had stormed into the school grounds and attacked pupils before running out again. If that was what everyone needed to tell themselves to stay sane, she was happy to let them think it. She might even start believing it herself one day.

"How did last night go?" asked Chris.

"Fine," said Alice. "I only woke up once. I fretted a bit, but that was more about mock exams rather than… what happened."

"It won't be long now," said Chris, squeezing her hand tighter. "You'll sleep right through the night and its face won't be there when you wake up."

Alice nodded. She didn't think she'd be much use to the troll now anyway. She had no more misery for it to feed off.

She felt her phone buzz in her pocket. So her dad had finally got round to replying to her last text.

It could wait. She was in no hurry.

THE END